Buster's Sugartime

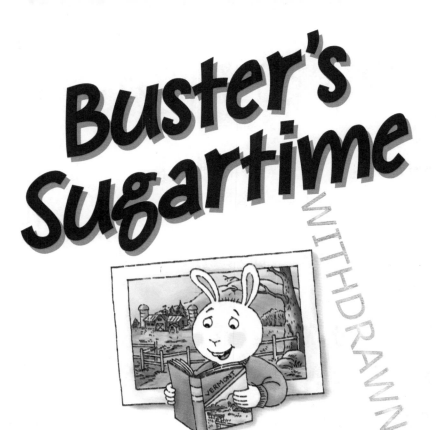

by Marc Brown

 LITTLE, BROWN AND COMPANY

New York ꙨＢoston

Copyright © 2006 by Marc Brown. All rights reserved.

Little, Brown and Company, Time Warner Book Group
1271 Avenue of the Americas, New York, NY 10020 • www.lb-kids.com
First Edition: April 2006
Library of Congress Cataloging-in-Publication Data
Brown, Marc Tolon.
Buster's sugartime / Marc Brown.—1st ed.   p. cm.—(Postcards from Buster)
Companion to the television program *Postcards from Buster*.
Summary: When his father takes him to visit Vermont, Buster sends postcards to his friends back home
telling them what he is learning about maple syrup and the "mud season."
ISBN 0-316-15915-8 (hc)—ISBN 0-316-00128-7 (pb)
[1. Maple syrup—Fiction. 2. Spring—Fiction. 3. Rabbits—Fiction. 4. Postcards—Fiction.
5. Vermont—Fiction.] I. Title. II. Series:Brown, Marc Tolon. Postcards from Buster. PZ7.B81618Bus 2006
[E]—dc22   2005010262

Printed in the United States of America • PHX • 10 9 8 7 6 5 4 3 2 1

All photos, except page 3, from the *Postcards from Buster* television series courtesy of WGBH Boston and Cookie Jar
Entertainment Inc. in association with Marc Brown Studios. Page 3, Karen Pike.

Do you know what these words MEAN?

bonfire: a large outdoor fire usually built as part of a celebration

drill: to make a hole in something by using a tool

gathered (GA-therd): collected or brought together

memory: something that happened to you that you will not forget

photographer (fuh-TAH-gruh-fer): a person who takes pictures with a camera

sap: gooey stuff that comes out of a tree

season (SEE-zun): a part of the year

tap: part of a tool used to take the sap out of a tree

Vermont

- The Green Mountains of Vermont are made up of 223 mountains.

- The first people to make maple syrup were Native Americans.

- It takes 30–50 gallons of sap to make one gallon of maple syrup.

- The state tree is the sugar maple.

"Buster, why are you packing
so many green clothes?"
Arthur asked.

"I'm going to Vermont," said Buster.
"It's the Green Mountain State."

"Vermont doesn't look very green right now," said Buster.

"This is mud season," his father explained. "It comes at the end of winter."

Dear Francine,

It's the middle of mud season here.

There's mud everywhere you look.

I bet they make lots of mud pies,
but I haven't seen any yet.

Buster

Francine Fre
Maple
Elwoo

Buster went to visit his mom's friends,
Karen and Gillian.
They had three children,
Emma, David, and James.

Dear D.W.,

I am visiting
a family
that has two dogs.

Scout is huge and
Sadie is tiny.

They would
have fun playing
with Pal.

Buster

Karen was a photographer.
Buster looked at some
of her pictures.

"You can tell a story
in pictures," he said,
"just like I do with my movies."

Later, Buster met Emma's friend Lily and her brother Taylor.

They were gathering logs for a bonfire.
Buster offered to help them.

Later, Buster met Emma's friend Lily
and her brother Taylor.

They were gathering logs for
a bonfire.
Buster offered to help them.

Dear Muffy,

I will see my first
bonfire tonight.
It will be set
in a deep pit
to be safe.

I think the fire
will be too big
to roast
marshmallows.

Buster

Emma and her friends took Buster to a store that sold sweet things made from maple syrup.

"This is my kind of place," said Buster.

Francin
Maple
Elwood City

A boy named Kameron
showed Buster
how to get syrup.
"First we drill the trunk," he said.

Buster hammered the tap
into the drilled hole.
"Is this maple syrup?" he asked.

"That's the sap," said Lily.

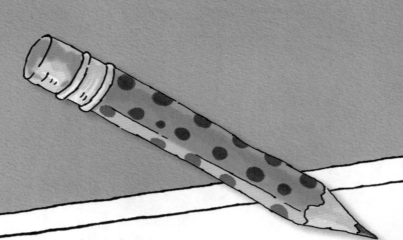

Dear Brain,

One tree does not make much sap for syrup.

But there are 2,500 trees here that send their sap to a big collector tank.

Then they boil off most of the water.

The syrup is what's left.

Buster

Alan
22 C
Elwc

That night Buster shared a dinner
with Emma's family and Lily's family.

Lily's moms, Tracy and Gina,
were very good cooks.

Dear Binky,

Have you ever
been stuffed with
macaroni and
cheese and
maple cheesecake?

It feels great as
long as you don't
have to move
afterward.

Buster

Later Karen gathered the
families for a picture.

"Say 'Buster'!" she told them
as she got the camera ready.

"BUSTER!" everyone shouted.
Click!

Then they all went to the bonfire.
The flames were warm and bright.

Dear Francine,

Mud season
in Vermont
may be a little
messy, but I think
you would like it.

And you get
a lot of exercise
wiping your feet
all the time.

Buster

"I want everyone to think
of their happiest winter memory,"
said Tracy.
"We're saying good-bye to winter,
and welcoming spring.
One, two, three—Good-bye, winter!"

Dear Everyone,

There's no
mud season here,
but we do have
maple trees.

If you come visit me,
we can find them and
have another sweet time.

Buster